Dear Parent:
Your child's love of reading starts here!

Every child learns to read in a different way and at his or her own speed. Some go back and forth between reading levels and read favorite books again and again. Others read through each level in order. You can help your young reader improve and become more confident by encouraging his or her own interests and abilities. From books your child reads with you to the first books he or she reads alone, there are I Can Read Books for every stage of reading:

SHARED READING
Basic language, word repetition, and whimsical illustrations, ideal for sharing with your emergent reader

BEGINNING READING
Short sentences, familiar words, and simple concepts for children eager to read on their own

READING WITH HELP
Engaging stories, longer sentences, and language play for developing readers

READING ALONE
Complex plots, challenging vocabulary, and high-interest topics for the independent reader

ADVANCED READING
Short paragraphs, chapters, and exciting themes for the perfect bridge to chapter books

I Can Read Books have introduced children to the joy of reading since 1957. Featuring award-winning authors and illustrators and a fabulous cast of beloved characters, I Can Read Books set the standard for beginning readers.

A lifetime of discovery begins with the magical words **"I Can Read!"**

Visit www.icanread.com for information
on enriching your child's reading experience.

I Can Read Book® is a trademark of HarperCollins Publishers.

Batman: The Joker's Ice Scream
Copyright © 2015 DC Comics.
BATMAN and all related characters and elements are trademarks of and © DC Comics.
(s15)

HARP33533

Library of Congress catalog card number: 2014958856
ISBN 978-0-06-234492-2

Book design by Victor Joseph Ochoa

16 17 18 19 20   LSCC   10 9 8 7 6   ❖   First Edition

BATMAN™

THE JOKER'S ICE SCREAM

by Donald Lemke
pictures by Andie Tong

Batman created by Bob Kane

HARPER
An Imprint of HarperCollinsPublishers

BATMAN

Batman is an expert martial artist, crime fighter, and inventor. He is also known as the Dark Knight.

COMMISSIONER JAMES GORDON

James Gordon is the Gotham City Police Commissioner. He works with Batman to stop crime in the city.

BATGIRL

Barbara Gordon fights alongside Batman, using high-tech gadgets and martial arts skills. Her father, James Gordon, does not know her secret identity as Batgirl.

BATMOBILE

The Batmobile is Batman's high-tech vehicle. It is protected by armor and filled with dozens of weapons and gadgets.

THE JOKER

The Joker is Batman's enemy and one of the most dangerous villains in Gotham City. His nickname is the Clown Prince of Crime.

HARLEY QUINN

Former doctor Harleen Frances Quinzel is the Joker's girlfriend and partner in crime.

In the Gotham City Police station, Commissioner James Gordon wiped sweat from his forehead. "Why's it so hot in here?" he asked. "The air conditioner is broken again, sir," answered an officer.

Gordon opened a nearby window.

The chimes of an ice cream truck

played on the street below.

"Time to cool off," he said

with a smile.

The green-and-purple truck
stopped in front of the station.
Painted on the side were two
big, bold words: ICE SCREAM!

A pale woman in a white hat greeted
the officers at the truck's window.
"What'll it be, boys?" she asked.
"I'll try a double scoop of
Vanilla Mean!" replied one officer.
"Kooky Dough for me!" said another.

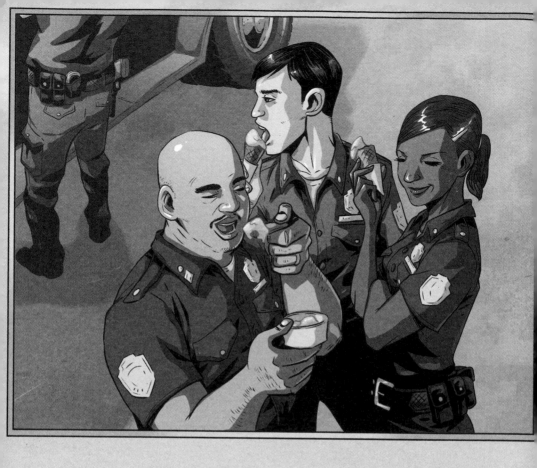

The woman quickly served up

the ice cream with a straight face.

"Hey," said an officer,

"your sign says 'service with a smile.'"

He took a lick of his cone.

The woman removed her white hat.

"And you'll get what you paid for!"

shouted Harley Quinn.

Suddenly the officer's mouth

stretched into a wide, wicked grin.

Soon every officer was smiling
and laughing uncontrollably.
"Look, Mr. J!" said Harley.
"You finally gave the police
something to smile about!"

"*I* tell the jokes," yelled the Joker

from the driver's seat.

"Now let's roll.

By the end of today,

every cop in this city

will be eating out of our hands."

Batman arrived in downtown Gotham City.
He stepped out of the Batmobile.
Empty ice cream cups littered the sidewalk.

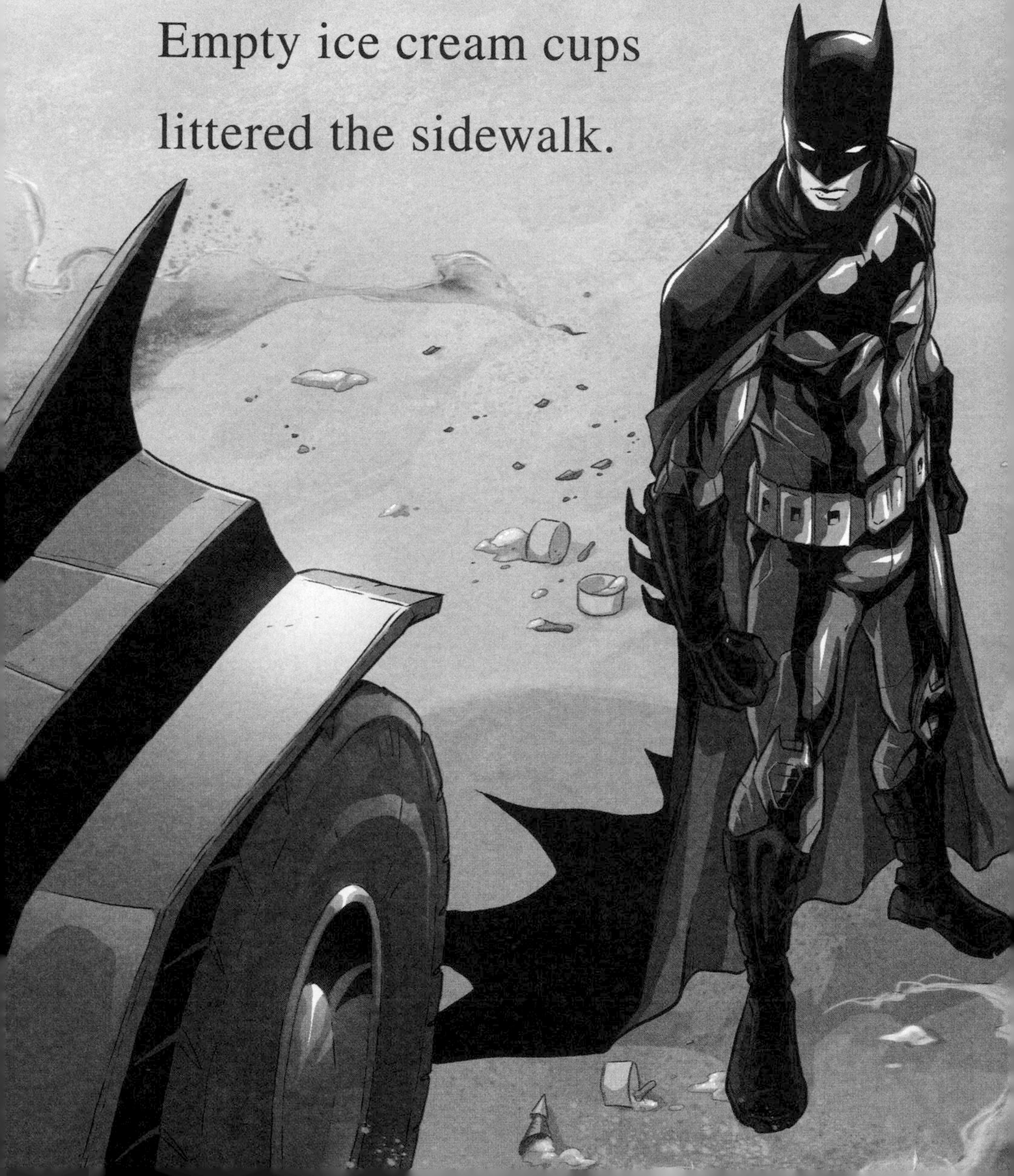

The Dark Knight kneeled next to
a half-eaten ice cream cone.
He removed a glass tube from
his Utility Belt and filled it
with some of the melted treat.
"Time to get the real scoop," he said.

Batman placed the tube

into a high-tech device

in the Batmobile.

The computer quickly identified

the formula: Joker Venom!

The poison left people with
a frozen smile and a craving
for more ice cream.

"If the Joker isn't stopped,"
said Batman, "the whole police force
will eat themselves silly!"

A few streets away,

the evil duo served up

their sweet treats.

Then Harley Quinn spotted the

Batmobile speeding toward them.

"It's Batman!" she cried.

The Joker pressed a large red button on the vehicle's dashboard.
In an instant, the ice cream truck changed into the Jokermobile.

The Joker led the Dark Knight on a
high-speed chase out of the city.
"He's gaining on us!" yelled Harley,
looking back at the Batmobile.
"I'll take care of him,"
said the Joker, "lickety-split!"

The villain pressed another button,
and the truck's rear doors opened.
Cherries, chocolate syrup, and bananas
spilled onto the road.

The Batmobile skidded in the
slippery sweets but stayed close.
"Time for seconds, Mr. J!"
Harley told her partner in crime.
"How about a little Rocky Road?"
the Joker said.
The villain steered the Jokermobile
onto a bumpy gravel road.
Soon the Batmobile was lost
in their dusty trail.

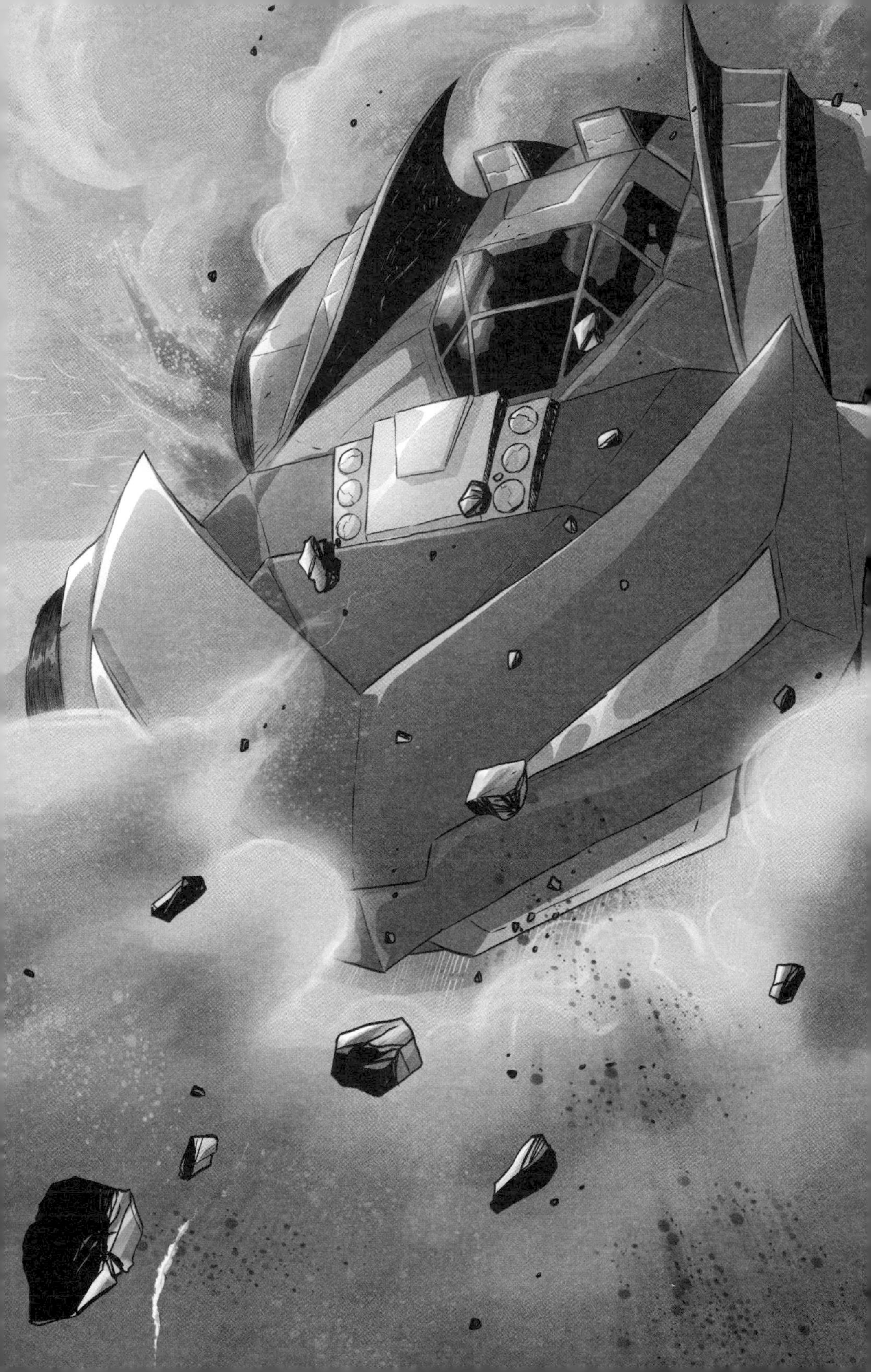

Suddenly a headlight appeared.
Batgirl blocked the road
on her Batcycle.
The hero flung a Batarang
at her enemies.

Boom! The Batarang exploded
in front of the Jokermobile.
"Look out, Mr. J!" cried Harley.
The truck crashed into the
explosion's cone-shaped crater.

Batman soon arrived at the scene.
"Thanks for helping me out
of a sticky situation," he said.
The heroes watched the villains
exit the Jokermobile.

Harley and the Joker were covered
from head to toe in ice cream!
"Looks like I'll be helping you
with another!" Batgirl laughed.

The heroes helped the evil duo
out of the pit.

"The joke's on you," said the Joker.

"The police still have a
case of brain freeze!"

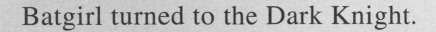

Batgirl turned to the Dark Knight.

"He's right," she said.

"How will we get

the antidote to the police?"

"On a hot day like this," he said,

"it's always best to keep cool."

The Batmobile returned
to Gotham City,
towing the Jokermobile behind.
A hungry crowd
quickly surrounded them.

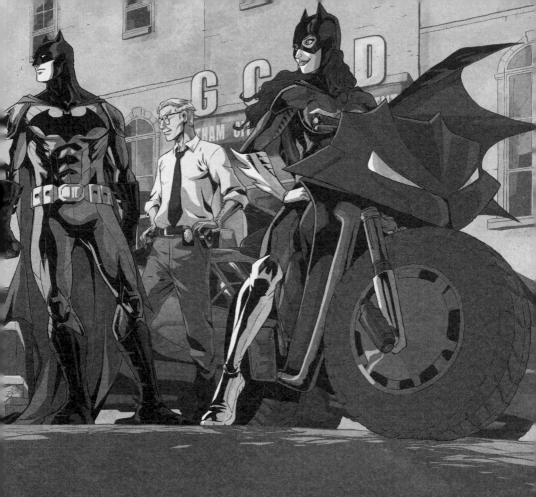

Harley and the Joker

served up their latest flavor.

It included a special ingredient:

the Joker Venom antidote!

Soon everyone was back to normal.

Batgirl zoomed off while Batman spoke to the commissioner.

"Question," Gordon said.

"What do you call this flavor?"

"Batswirl," Batman said.

"A Dynamic Duo!"

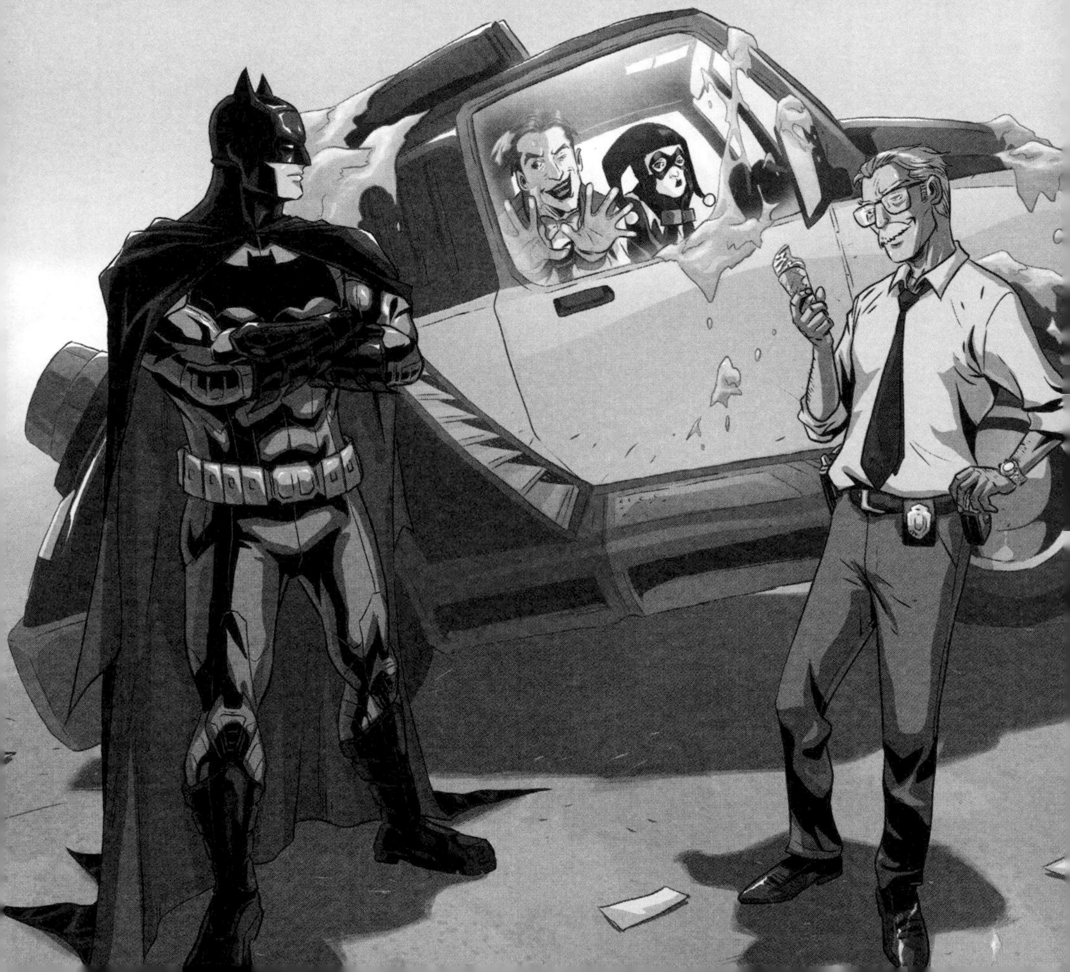